LOVE PEANUT HEAD

by Pete Johnson

TO JAN, LINDA AND ROBIN,
AND BILL BLOOMFIELD.

Illustrated by David Parkin

Scott

Andy

Hi, it's Scott here. How are you doing? I'm
fourteen and I've never been in trouble at
school – until now.

It was Andy who started all the trouble.
He was a mate from my class. We got on well.
Then he did something which made me jump in
the air – with pain. But it was an accident.

If only Peanut Head hadn't found out.
Who is Peanut Head? He is the world's most
frightening headmaster. He's a monster!

But I made Peanut Head very angry.
You won't believe what I did. I still can't
believe it myself.
Let me tell you what happened ...

Chapter 1

I'm in big trouble. Do you want to know why?

It all started in CDT. I was beating away at a bit of hot metal. That's a brilliant laugh. You get these huge orange sparks. And the harder you hit, the higher the sparks fly.

I was putting my metalwork in the fire, next to Andy Doyle's, when it happened.

Andy Doyle just turned round and swung his poker right into my elbow.

Suddenly, I was the world's greatest disco dancer, twisting and jumping about in the air. I tell you, the pain was terrible. It felt as if Andy Doyle was still pressing that poker against my elbow.

Actually, Andy was staring at me as if
he couldn't believe his eyes. Then I heard
someone shout, "Andy's just stabbed
Scott." At once the whole class was
crowding around me.

Mr Ferguson, the metalwork teacher, was called Fungus – because he had smelly armpits. He was down in the stockroom.

We reckoned he was having a crafty fag.

"I'll hear any noise," he said. He always said that. But he never did.

Andy asked me, "Are you all right, mate?"

A bit of a stupid question, really. So I just nodded.

I looked down at the sleeve of my grey jersey. Clouds of smoke were still coming off it. There was a very big hole. The edges of the hole had gone all black. The black looked like treacle, and my white shirt had strange brown stuff over it.

Everyone wanted to see my burn. They were sorry there was no blood. But my skin had gone all white and funny. And there was a large pink spot in the middle of my elbow. Water was oozing out of that pink spot now. And it hurt like crazy.

"Thanks a lot, Andy. You big prat," I said. Actually, Andy wasn't big at all. He was short and skinny with ginger hair.

"You've trashed my shirt and jersey," I cried.

He grinned at me. "At least you won't have to wear your tacky nylon shirt any more. You should thank me for that."

Some of the boys started laughing. That got me so mad, I punched Andy on the shoulder. I didn't hit him very hard.

But I had surprised him. He was sweating now. Then he said, very quietly, "Look, I'm sorry, all right?" I don't think anyone else heard him. But I did.

I said, "It's OK. I'll dump my shirt and jersey and tell my mum they got stolen out of my locker or ... I'll think of something."

It was sorted. It was over.

Chapter 2

Then the door opened and we heard a voice say, "What's going on? What are you all looking at?"

Oh no! The Headmaster. Trust him to come in now.

The Headmaster walked over to me, then sniffed loudly. "I can smell burning. What is it?"

At first, no one answered. Then Andy Doyle said, "I think it's Mr Ferguson, Sir."

"Mr Ferguson?" snapped the Headmaster.

"Yes, Sir. I think he's in the stockroom having a cigarette," said Andy. This made

everyone want to laugh. But no one dared.

There was silence. Everyone was quietly moving away. "Don't waste my time," snapped the Headmaster. "Come on, who did this?"

"It was an accident," began Andy. "I just turned round and didn't see ..."

"What's your name?" cried the Headmaster.

"Andrew Doyle, Sir," he said.

"Go and wait outside my room." He turned to me. "You, go to my room, too."

Then Fungus appeared. He went red when he saw the Headmaster. But I didn't hear what the Headmaster said to him. I was too busy bricking it. Not even the hardest boys in the school messed with the Headmaster.

We walked over to the Headmaster's room. He was right behind us. I could feel the tips of his fingers on my shoulders. It was as if he was pushing me along.

"You first," he said to me.

17

Chapter 3

Inside his office, the Headmaster plonked himself down on a chair. It had wheels so you could ride around the room on it. I'd have loved one of those.

The Headmaster was bald, with little round glasses, and he had a very small head. That's why we called him Peanut Head. "Tell me exactly what happened," said Peanut Head.

"Well, Sir ..." I stuttered. "Andy walked into me, but it was nobody's fault."

"Don't be stupid, boy," roared the Headmaster. Then he grabbed me by the arm and yelled, "Who did this?"

Who did this?

"It was an accident, Sir. But it doesn't matter because my arm doesn't hurt any more."

Actually, the pain was still running up and down my arm.

I looked hopefully at Peanut Head. But he just asked, "What's your name?"

"Scott Peterson, Sir."

"Yes, well, Peterson, be sure and see Nurse on your way out, won't you?" He started to look angry. "And send Doyle in."

I got up. "I am feeling really well now, Sir. And my mum was going to throw that jersey out anyway. So Andy just saved her the trouble, really." I smiled nervously.

Peanut Head sighed. "Send Doyle in," he said again. I crept away.

Later that day, Andy Doyle ran over to me. "Thanks a lot," he said. "You really grassed me up."

"No, I didn't," I said.

"Oh, no? Well, how come Peanut Head said it was all my fault?"

"But I told him it was just an accident," I said.

"Yeah, it really sounds like it. And thanks to you, I've got to clean the desks after school for two hours. Cheers, mate."

He charged off. I went after him, but he wouldn't listen. And then, to be honest, I got a bit fed up with him.

After all, I was the one with the trashed clothes and the dirty great blister.

Chapter 4

Next morning, my mum said my only
other white shirt was dirty, and I'd have to
wear a bright red shirt to school.

I said, "Mum, when Peanut Head sees
me, he'll go mad."

But my mum just said, "They won't tell
you off, not after what's happened."

So, it was the end of assembly and
we were all leaving the hall, when Peanut
Head called out, "Scott Peterson."

Now I'm really going to get it, I
thought. But instead, something worse
happened. Much, much worse.

Peanut Head patted me on the back, gave me a false grin and said, "I hope your arm is better, Scott." And we walked out of assembly together. I turned bright red.

Andy Doyle saw the whole thing. Soon he was spreading it around the school. And he stuck this bit of paper on my back, saying:

I didn't find it until break-time. Then he got people to come up to me and say stupid things like, "Aren't you going to take Peanut Head a cup of tea, then?"

27

At lunch-time, his mates kept trying to push me out of the queue. It was so stupid. But they all thought I'd grassed Andy up to Peanut Head.

What a mess. I had to talk to Andy again. So I sat at the same table as him at lunch-time. But then Peanut Head came

towards us, his tray in his hand. We
always have to leave a space at the top of
the table for teachers. So I said, "I hope
Peanut Head's not going to sit here."

"Don't lie," said Andy Doyle. "He's
your chum. I bet you'll be going home
with him tonight."

"Don't talk rubbish," I said. I looked down and picked up the salt. Then I heard a tray clang on to the table. The table started to shake as a chair was pulled out. It was the only sound on the table. Everyone stopped talking.

I turned, and out of the corner of my eye, I saw Peanut Head. I watched him take all the food off his tray, pushing his treacle pudding to one side. Then he started laying out his knife and fork – teachers always take hours doing that sort of thing.

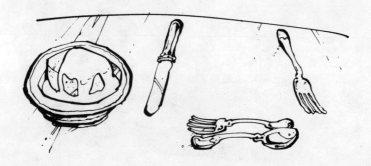

He looked up, spotted me and said, "Ah, hello, Scott, so what lesson have you just had?"

"Geography, Sir," I croaked.

"Geography, eh? That's interesting, isn't it?" he said.

"Yes, Sir." I started pouring salt over my meal. My face was burning.

Then Peanut Head got up to put his tray away. Teachers always make a big show of putting their trays away; they think it is setting a good example.

"Just can't keep away from you, can he?" said Andy. Then he started copying the way I'd said, "Geography, Sir." The whole table laughed.

Chapter 5

I had to show I wasn't Peanut Head's pet.
But how? I could just leave. No, I must *do*
something. But what?

Then I saw I had the answer in my
hand. I unscrewed the top of the salt so it
was really loose.

Everyone watched me in silence. I think I'd shocked them – even Andy Doyle. One girl said, "You're mad," and left. Two boys followed. The only ones left were Andy Doyle, another guy who reckoned he was hard, and me.

Then Peanut Head returned. I saw his hand reach for the jug of water. He had fat fingers with large black hairs all over them. One of his fingernails was totally black.

"So what have you been doing in
geography today, Scott?"

"Rocks, Sir," I mumbled.

He didn't hear me. He was too busy
yelling across the dining room, "You, girl!
What on earth have you got on your legs?"
Everyone in the dining hall just froze.

"Yes, you, girl. How dare you wear
purple tights to school? Go and wait
outside my room, NOW." Peanut Head
was so cross, he spat the words across the
room. Some of the spit stuck to his lips.
I was scared now. I didn't want Peanut
Head spitting at me.

His right hand was moving down the table. We all stared at it. He picked up his beaker of water. I started to breathe again.

Maybe he wouldn't use any salt today.

"I hope you're all going to be watching our rugby team tonight," said Peanut Head.

"I'm already booked," said Andy Doyle. "I've got a detention tonight, Sir." Peanut Head gave Andy a really dirty look. Then he snatched up the salt. Andy Doyle kicked me under the table. I was so terrified, I couldn't even swallow.

Peanut Head started to shake the salt. At once, the top dropped off, bounced on to the side of the plate and fell, splat, into the gravy. A mountain of salt was pouring on to his plate. Soon there was a white snowdrift all over his meal, and what looked like a snowman was sitting on top of his potatoes.

Peanut Head looked totally amazed. He was breathing heavily. There were specks of gravy all over his tie. I caught Andy Doyle's eye. He grinned at me.

Peanut Head roared down the table,
"Get that grin off your face, boy." He
marched over to where Andy was sitting.
He stood right behind Andy. Then he
grabbed him by the shoulders. "So you
think this is funny, do you, boy?"

Andy could hardly speak. "No ... NO ... Sir," he gasped.

He pulled Andy to his feet. "You are in deep trouble," he said.

That's when I very shakily got up. "Sir, I did it." But I don't think Peanut Head heard me. So I said it again. "Sir, it was me. I did it, not Andy."

Now Peanut Head *did* look at me. His face was bright red and all the veins on his neck were sticking out. "Ah, yes, Peterson. I can trust you," he said. "Take my plate to Mrs Edwards and ask her very nicely if the Headmaster can have another meal sent to his room."

I stared at him. He was so angry, he hadn't heard me. Then he yelled, "What are you waiting for, Peterson?" But before I could reply, he and Andy had gone.

Chapter 6

So Andy Doyle got told to clean the desks every Friday, for a month. He had to start that day. Well, there was only one thing

for me to do, wasn't there? I had to do Andy Doyle's punishment for him. Luckily, the cleaners didn't know any of our names.

Anyway, I had just finished when a voice boomed down the corridor. "Is Andrew Doyle behaving himself?"

I tried turning my back, but there was no hiding that red shirt. Peanut Head knew me at once. And he was so shocked he could hardly speak at first.

Now the story continues outside Peanut Head's office at nine o'clock on Monday. Andy Doyle's got to be there too.

Wish me luck, won't you?